CU00942742

About the Author

Francesca Sheehan is mother and first-time author of the children's picture book *I'm Hiding From My Mummy*. When the world came to a halt, Francesca took the opportunity to work towards achieving a dream of hers. By combining her love for creative writing with her two young children as inspiration, she has put pen to paper and written her debut children's picture book.

I'm Hiding From
My Mummy

Francesca Sheehan

I'm Hiding From My Mummy

Nightingale Books

NIGHTINGALE PAPERBACK

© Copyright 2022
Francesca Sheehan

The right of Francesca Sheehan to be identified as author of
this work has been asserted by her in accordance with the
Copyright, Designs and Patents Act 1988.

All Rights Reserved

No reproduction, copy or transmission of this publication
may be made without written permission.
No paragraph of this publication may be reproduced,
copied or transmitted save with the written permission of the publisher, or in accordance
with the provisions of the Copyright Act 1956 (as amended).

Any person who commits any unauthorised act in relation to
this publication may be liable to criminal
prosecution and civil claims for damages.

A CIP catalogue record for this title is
available from the British Library.
ISBN 978-1-83875-338-2

Nightingale Books is an imprint of
Pegasus Elliot MacKenzie Publishers Ltd.
www.pegasuspublishers.com

First Published in 2022

Nightingale Books
Sheraton House Castle Park
Cambridge England

Printed & Bound in Great Britain

Dedication

For Evelyn-Rose and Luca.
Forever my inspiration and motivation.

Acknowledgements

Mum and Dad, thank you.

I'm hiding from my mummy,
We're playing hide and seek.
She's counting up to ten and
I've told her not to peek.

I know that she won't find me,
I'm hiding very low.
I'm lying in an igloo,
Made of fluffy, white snow.

It's chilly all around me,
There is frost between my toes,
And a long, shimmering icicle
Is hanging from my nose!

With penguins to my left
And polar bears to my right.
If Mummy doesn't find me,
I might stay overnight!

I'm going to get warm and comfy,
And maybe rest my eyes,
But as I do, my mum appears,
Much to my surprise.

How did you find me, Mummy?
Please can we play again?
You won't find me this time, Mummy,
So go and count to ten.

I'm hiding from my mummy,
We're playing hide and seek.
She's counting up to ten and
I've told her not to peek.

I know that she won't find me,
I'm being really brave,
Because this time I'm hiding
In a deep and dark cave.

There's darkness all around me,
The cave is eerie and black.
I think that I can feel a spider
Crawling up my back!

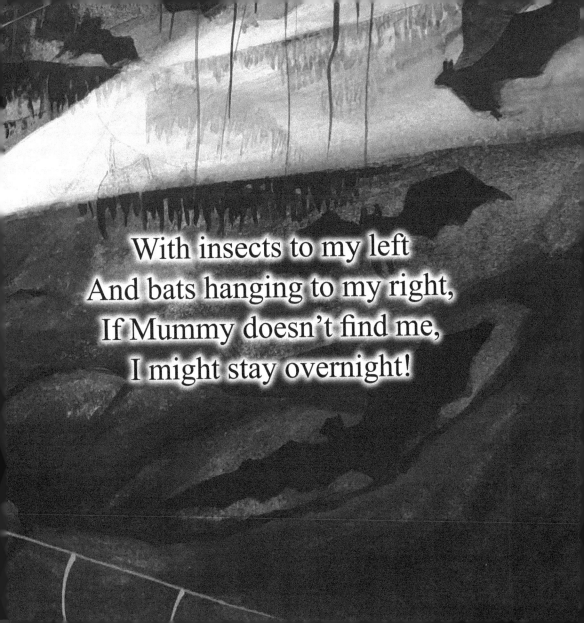

With insects to my left
And bats hanging to my right,
If Mummy doesn't find me,
I might stay overnight!

I'm going to get warm and comfy,
And maybe rest my eyes,
But as I do, my mum appears,
Much to my surprise.

How did you find me, Mummy?
Please can we play again?
You won't find me this time, Mummy,
So go and count to ten.

I'm hiding from my mummy,
we're playing hide and seek.
She's counting up to ten and
I've told her not to peek.

I know that she won't find me,
You all just wait and see.
I'm hiding in the jungle,
Behind a towering palm tree.

Thick forest all around me,
I hear a parrot's call.
Over there's an enormous elephant
Standing strong and tall.

With tigers to my left
And gorillas to my right,
If Mummy doesn't find me,
I might stay overnight!

I'm going to get warm and comfy,
And maybe rest my eyes,
But as I do, my mum appears,
Much to my surprise.

How did you find me, Mummy?
Please can we play again?
You won't find me this time, Mummy,
So go and count to ten.

I'm hiding from my mummy,
We're playing hide and seek.
She's counting up to ten and
I've told her not to peek.

Now, this place is soft and cosy,
I'm somewhere very snug.
I'm happy and safe tucked up in here,
No snow, or trees, or bugs!

I'm going to get warm and comfy,
And maybe rest my eyes,
Slowly drifting off to sleep,
The perfect place to hide.